Looking for the best?
Look for the Bear!

CANDLEWICK PRESS

Good Night Like This

Mary Murphy

Yawny
and dozy,
twitchy
and cozy.

Good night,
rabbits.

Sleep tight....

Flitty and shiny,
flashy and
tiny.

Good night,
Fireflies.
Sleep tight...

Quiet and strong
all winter long.

Good night,
bears.
sleep tight...

Tickly
and feathery
in any old
weathery.

Good night,
ducks.
Sleep tight...

like
this.

Good night!

Snorey
and furry,
stretchy
and purry.

Good night, cats.
Sleep tight...

Swoosh, swish,
make a
bedtime wish.

Good night, mice.
Sleep tight...

like
this.

Look! Everyone's all tucked up in bed. Now it's your turn, sleepyhead.

So, good night,
you.
Sleep tight . . .